The
GLOVE PUPPET MAN

John Yeoman

Illustrated by

Emma Chichester Clark

Collins

An Imprint of HarperCollinsPublishers

First published in hardback in Great Britain by
HarperCollins Publishers Ltd in 1997
1 3 5 7 9 10 8 6 4 2
ISBN 0 00 198142 0
Text copyright © John Yeoman 1997
Illustrations copyright © Emma Chichester Clark 1997
The author and illustrator assert the moral right to be identified as the author and illustrator of this work.
A CIP catalogue record for this book is available from the British Library.
77-85 Fulham Palace Road, Hammersmith, London W6 8JB
Printed and bound in Hong Kong

The Glove Puppet Man got up nice and early, as usual, had a quick breakfast, and put on Left-Hand Pig and Right-Hand Pig.

"Come on, Pigs," he said. "Time to go to the market square."

But what a shock he had when he went to the rickety shed to collect his puppet theatre. The roof had collapsed in the night and his beautiful theatre was completely ruined. Left-Hand Pig and Right-Hand Pig threw up their trotters in dismay.

"This is terrible," gasped the Glove Puppet Man. "Unless Mrs Smiley has a puppet theatre on her second-hand stall we shan't be able to give our play. We must hurry!"

A few minutes later he saw Miss Prim on her hands
and knees beside the hedge, looking very glum.

"I've lost the new earrings I was going to wear at
the party tonight," she sighed. "Whatever can I do?"

"Come with me to Mrs Smiley's second-hand stall,"
said the Glove Puppet Man; "she's sure to have some."

And off they went.

A few minutes later they saw Mr Loam in his barnyard, staring at a miserable peacock.

"This peacock of mine has lost all his beautiful tail feathers," he moaned, "and it's upset him dreadfully. Where can I get some more?"

"Come with us to Mrs Smiley's second-hand stall," said the Glove Puppet Man; "she's sure to have some."

And off they went.

A few minutes later they saw the little Tuffet twins sitting on a swing in the park.

"The dog has run away with our skipping rope," they sobbed, "and we wanted to go skipping this morning. Where can we find another?"

"Come with us to Mrs Smiley's second–hand stall," said
the Glove Puppet Man; "she's sure to have one."
And off they went.

A few minutes later they saw
Mr Sparkle at the pump, with two
pieces of ladder in his hands.
"My ladder's got woodworm and it's broken
in half," he grumbled. "How on earth can I clean
anybody's top windows now?"
"Come with us to Mrs Smiley's second-hand stall,"
said the Glove Puppet Man; "she's sure to have one."
And off they went.

A few minutes later they saw Master Blast on the bandstand, holding a flattened piece of metal.

"That carthorse has just stepped on my trombone," he blubbered, "and unless I can buy another I won't be able to play in the band this evening. How can I manage?"

"Come with us to Mrs Smiley's second-hand stall," said the Glove Puppet Man; "she's sure to have one."

And off they went.

A few minutes later they saw Mrs Sudds down by the river with a basket of wet washing on her head.

"My clothesline has snapped in two," she cried, "and I don't know how I'm going to get my washing dry this afternoon."

"Come with us to Mrs Smiley's second-hand stall,"
said the Glove Puppet Man; "she's sure to have one."
And off they went.

A few minutes later they saw Mr Bellow, the town crier, on the steps of the Town Hall. He was holding up a woolly scarf full of holes.

"I need to keep my neck well wrapped up so that I don't get a sore throat," he muttered, "and the moths have ruined my scarf. Wherever can I get another?"

"Come with us to Mrs Smiley's second-hand stall," said the Glove Puppet Man; "she's sure to have one."

And off they went.

A few minutes later they
saw Miss Pamper, the nursemaid,
sitting on a bench in the rose alley.
She had a baby on one knee and a torn
baby sling on the other.

"The bottom's ripped out of this baby sling,"
she wailed, "and if I have to hold the baby
how can I get on with my knitting?"

"Come with us to Mrs Smiley's
second-hand stall," said the
Glove Puppet Man; "she's
sure to have one."

And off they went.

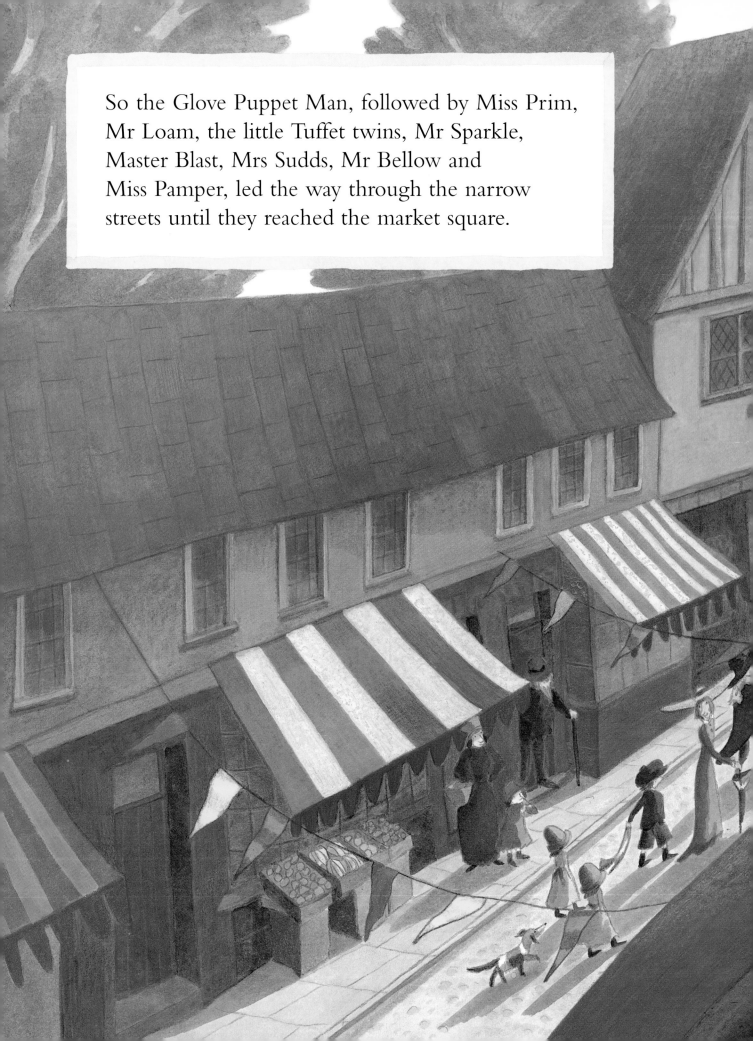

So the Glove Puppet Man, followed by Miss Prim,
Mr Loam, the little Tuffet twins, Mr Sparkle,
Master Blast, Mrs Sudds, Mr Bellow and
Miss Pamper, led the way through the narrow
streets until they reached the market square.

There was Mrs Smiley's second-hand stall in its usual place.

"I hope we find what we want for everybody. Including me," said the Glove Puppet Man. And Left-Hand Pig and Right-Hand Pig nodded.

Mrs Smiley was very pleased to see them all. But when she heard what they wanted, she looked sad.

"I'm truly sorry I can't help anybody," she said, "but this is all I've got left. And when I've sold everything I'm giving up the stall to take a rest."

And she showed them: a cracked washbasin, a kite,
two springs, a sleepy snake, two pushchair wheels, a
big bunch of artificial flowers, a string of sausages and
an old wind-up gramophone.

Everybody looked disappointed. Except the
Glove Puppet Man.

He fastened the pushchair
wheels on to Miss Prim's ears.

"What a beautiful pair
of earrings they make,"
she said.

Miss Prim admired
herself in Mrs Smiley's
cracked mirror.

He tied the bunch of artificial
flowers on to Mr Loam's peacock.

"Doesn't he look smart
now!" said Mr Loam.

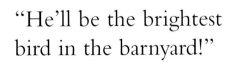

"He'll be the brightest
bird in the barnyard!"

He gave each of the Tuffet twins one end of the string of sausages.

"This will do marvellously for a skipping rope until the dog brings ours back," said the twins. "Then he can have the sausages."

He attached the two springs to
the bottom of Mr Sparkle's shoes.

"This solves my problem," said Mr Sparkle. "I can bounce up and down and clean the highest window without a ladder now!"

He showed Master Blast how to blow down the pipe
of the washbasin and make sounds by turning the tap.
   "What a terrific noise," said Master Blast. "I bet
they ask me to march in front of the band this evening."

He pegged Mrs Sudds' washing on to the tail
of the kite and sent it flying into the air.

"That will dry it wonderfully," said
Mrs Sudds, "and give me something
to amuse the children with while
I'm waiting."

He wound the sleepy snake round Mr Bellow's throat.
   "What a warm and cosy scarf it makes," said
Mr Bellow. "And it'll never get the moths."

He tied the gramophone round Miss Pamper's shoulders
and popped the baby into the horn.

"How very kind," said Miss Pamper. "Now the baby
can see everything that's going on and I can finish my
knitting."

"Wonderful!" cried Mrs Smiley, clapping her hands. "Everybody's got what they wanted!" Then she looked serious. "Except you," she said.

The Glove Puppet Man thought for a moment, and Left-Hand Pig and Right-Hand Pig scratched their heads.

"I know!" he exclaimed. "I'll buy your stall since you don't need it any more. If you would all kindly lend a hand we can make it into a perfect puppet theatre!"

And in no time at all they'd stood the stall on its end and rearranged the drapes so that it turned into a puppet theatre.
 And before they all went off home the Glove Puppet Man got Left-Hand Pig and Right-Hand Pig to entertain them with a wonderful show.

THE END